For you, Nicole Tugeau, and for all you do.

ISBN 978-0-7624-4354-3
Library of Congress Control Number: 2011934616

E-book ISBN 978-0-7624-4511-0

9 8 7 6 5 4 3 2 1
Digit on the right indicates the number of this printing

Designed by Ryan Hayes
Edited by Lisa Cheng
Typography: Typography of Coop

Published by Running Press Kids
An Imprint of Running Press Book Publishers
A Member of the Perseus Books Group
2300 Chestnut Street
Philadelphia, PA 19103–4371

Visit us on the web!
www.runningpress.com

SOUP FOR ONE

by Ethan Long

RP KIDS
PHILADELPHIA · LONDON

Tee hee hee!
Some soup for me!

1

Shoo, fly, shoo!
It's not for **two!**

I hope you see,
it won't seat **three!**

3

No more! No more!
It won't hold **four!**

I won't survive
if there are **five!**

5

I'm in a fix!
Look out for **six**!

Oh, good heavens!
Not soup for **seven!**

Great! Just great!
Here comes **eight**!

I hate to dine
in groups of **nine**.

Not again!
Now there are **ten!**

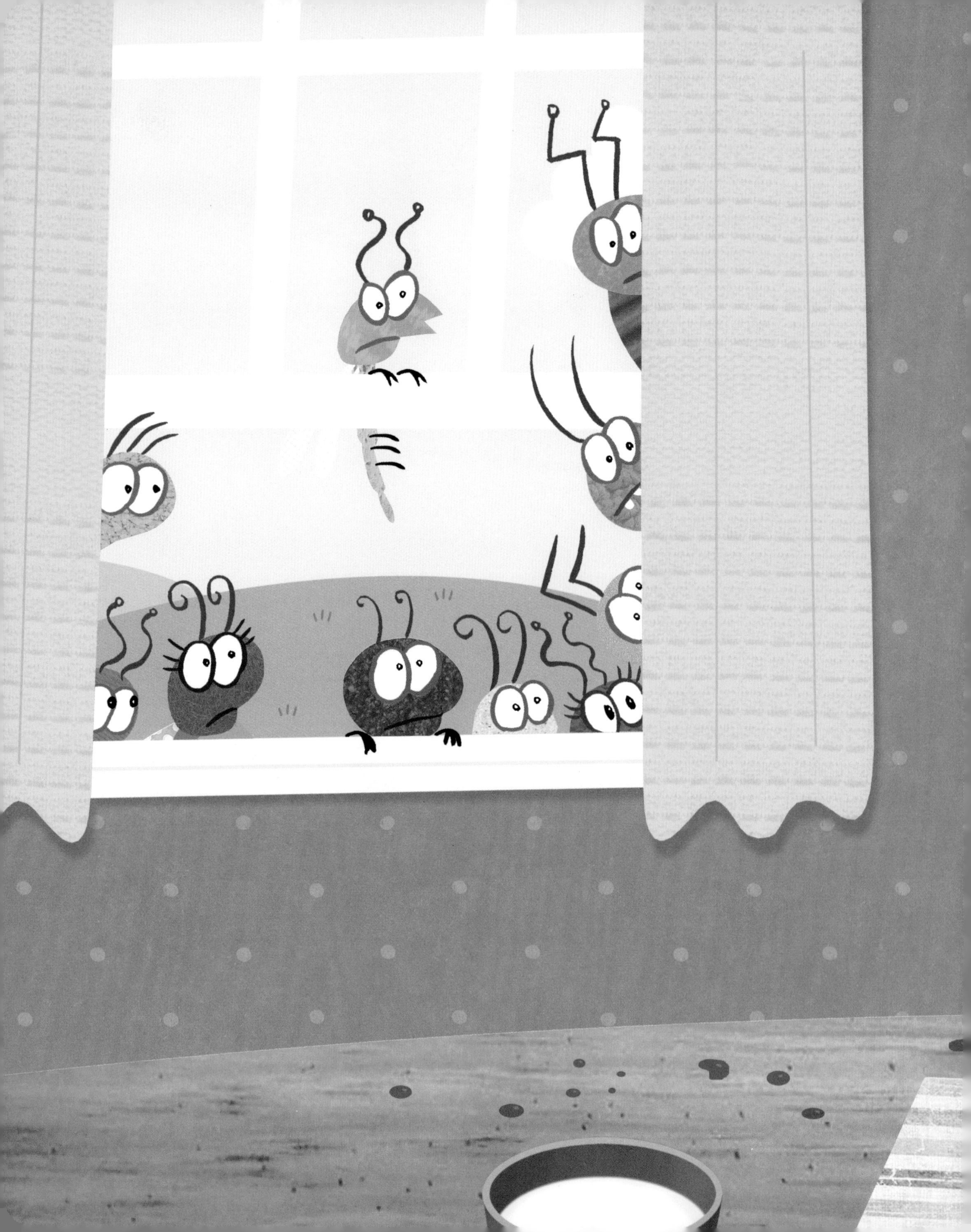

HE WANTS DESSERT!

Finally! They're done!

MMMMMM!
Soup for one!

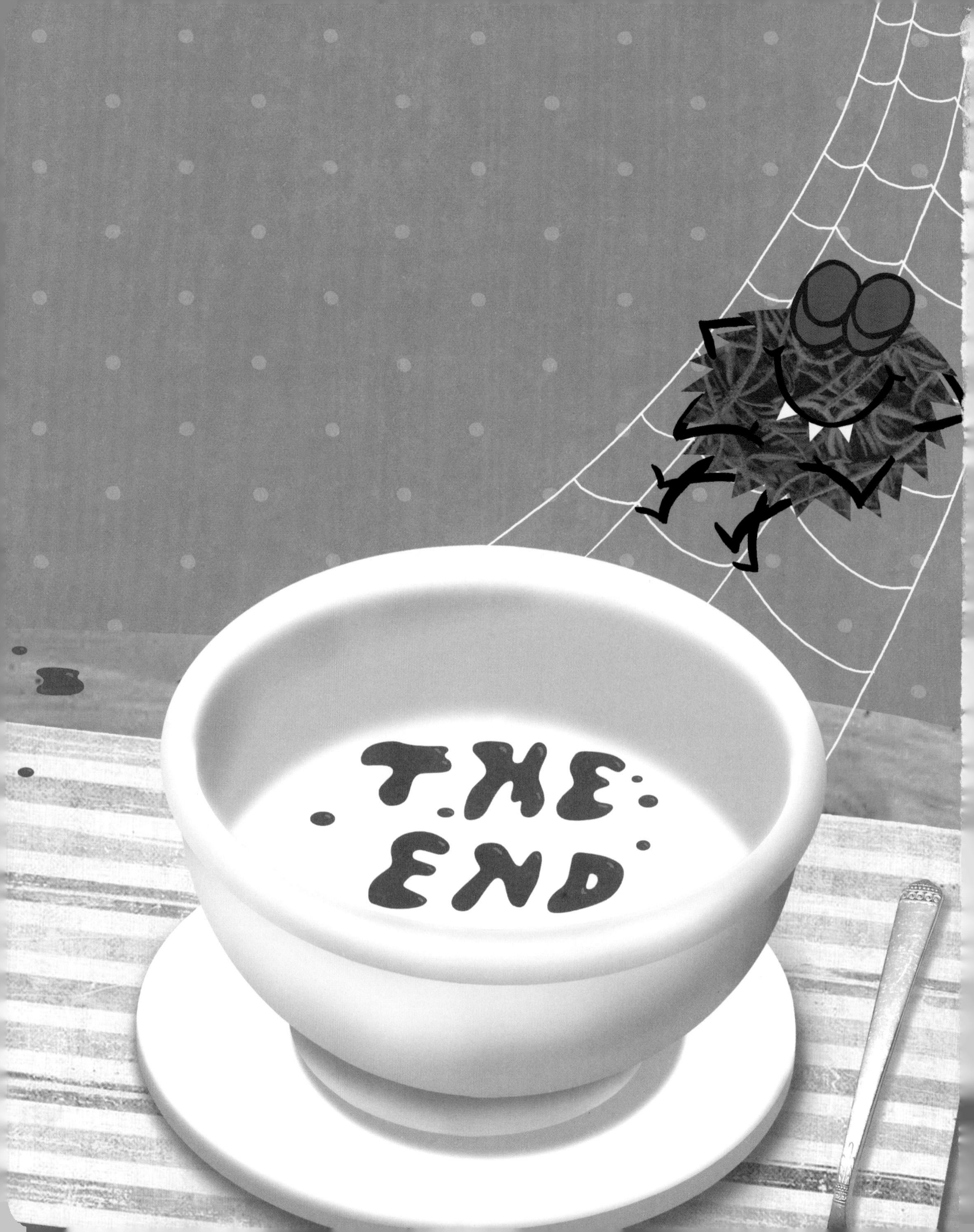
THE
END

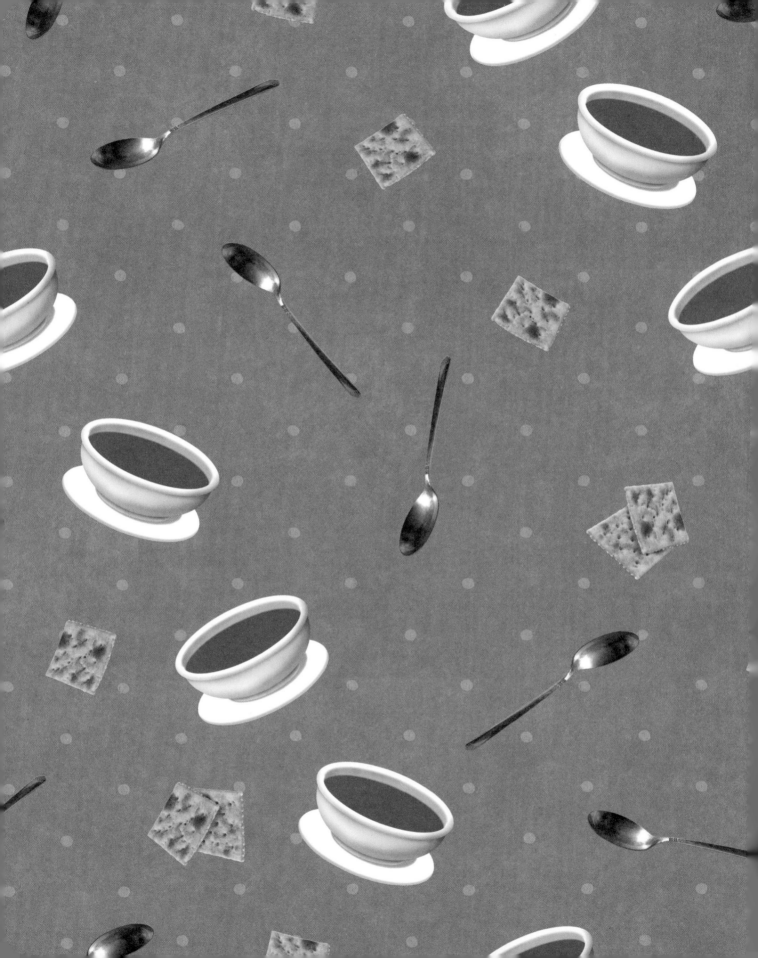